REASONS TO
WRITE RHYMES

REASONS TO WRITE RHYMES

Rob Bradley

Rob Bradley

A COLLECTION OF RAPS AND RHYMING POETRY FROM
ROB BRADLEY

First published in Great Britain in 2019
by Caboodle Book Ltd
Copyright © Rob Bradley 2019

A Catalogue record for this book is available
from the British Library.

ISBN 978-1-9997749-4-3

Illustrations by Joseph Witchall
Page Layout by Joseph Witchall
Printed and bound by CPI Group (UK) Ltd, Croydon, CR0 4YY

The paper and board used in the paperback by
Caboodle Books Ltd are natural recycleable products
made from wood grown in sustainable forests.
The manufacturing processes conform to the environmental
regulations of the country of origin.

Caboodle Books Ltd
Riversdale, 8 Rivock Avenue, Steeton, BD20 6SA
www.authorsabroad.com

CONTENTS

CONTENTS

REASON 1

...BECAUSE
SOME THOUGHTS
KEEP YOU
AWAKE AT NIGHT

SOMETHING TO THINK ABOUT

What are thoughts?
Are they real?
What are they made of?
How do they feel?

We have so many
In any given day
When one appears
Can you think it away?

We pull our thoughts
Out of thin air
We think of a thought
Then, like magic, it's there

Do two different people
With two different minds
Ever think the same thought
At the very same time?

Have you ever wondered
If someone somewhere
Is thinking of you now
And you're unaware?

Some thoughts show up
And it isn't a choice
Like an unwelcome stranger
A trespassing voice

Sometimes it's a gift
When a thought just appears
Like a flash of lightning
A life-changing idea

If you were to add up
Each one of your thoughts
Would there be a million,
A billion or more?

At times what we think
Is not what we say
We swallow our secrets
And hide them away

Some linger a while
Some drift like a cloud
Now, isn't all that something
To think about?

(ANTI) SOCIAL MEDIA

We are the generation
brought up online
always connected
all of the time

With phones, that we don't
really use like phones
super computers
we've fused to our bones

Impressed on our palms
our fingers flicking
and clicking
this is digital addiction

Tweeting, liking,
commenting, sharing
envying, trolling,
obsessing, comparing

Maybe we've swallowed
a parasite
Our feed isn't filling
our huge appetites

Any bus, any train,
any bench, any town
shoulders hunch over
and heads hang down

The real world
suddenly doesn't exist
silence spreads like
a thick morning mist

Our social networks
have grown to be global
but somehow
it feels so anti-social

TIME

Whether I'm asleep or awake

You keep on going.   Keep on going.   Keep on.

Whether I'm working or on a break

You keep on going.   Keep on going.   Keep on.

Even when it feels like you stop

You keep on going.   Keep on going.   Keep on.

You're still going round the clock

You keep on going.   Keep on going.   Keep on.

When I was a baby you crawled

You keep on going.   Keep on going.   Keep on.

Now you march on and don't stall

You keep on going.   Keep on going.   Keep on.

It's funny how you're always here

You keep on going.   Keep on going.   Keep on.

Yet you always disappear

You keep on going.   Keep on going.   Keep on.

Going.

ORION'S BELT

It's funny how stars
put it all in perspective
'cause they're about as far away
as something can be

And you can be distant
from something close
I don't know the last time
I saw my family

I tilt my head
to the sky for help
and I'm distracted
by Orion's belt

Everytime I think
I'm by myself
it reminds me that they
share this sky as well

AN IDIOM'S GUIDE TO CONTRADICTION

If '*many hands make light work*', is it true

that '*too many cooks spoil the broth*' too?

If '*actions speak louder that words*' is it flawed

to say that '*the pen's mightier than the sword*'?

And you '*shouldn't judge a book by its cover*'
correct?

then please explain how '*what you see is what you get*'

If '*the early bird catches the worm*' don't be late

but remember '*good things come to those who wait*'

REASON 2

...BECAUSE YOU ARE THE BEST PERSON TO TELL YOUR STORY

MY NOSE

What smells but has no odour?
My nose
What's boneless but can be broken?
My nose
What doesn't need cutting to bleed?
My nose
What runs but doesn't have feet?
My nose
What snorts and sneezes?
My nose
What whistles and wheezes?
My nose
What needs to be blown when it's blocked?
My nose
What itches when it's close to dogs?
My nose
What turns red in winter?
My nose
What's picked by my finger?
My nose

What's sharp as the fin of a shark?
My nose
What makes me look like an aardvark?
My nose
What's the first thing you see on my face?
My nose
What did my first girlfriend want to change?
My nose
What's the reason I was mocked in school?
My nose
What's the opposite of minuscule?
My nose
What's passed down from my mum's side?
My nose
What makes all my family alike?
My nose
But what do I secretly love?
My nose
So really ... it's no skin off
My nose

6.45 AT THE SHOP

SLAP in the middle
of a pebble-dashed maze
of semi-detached homes
that all look the same

There's a row of four shops
in a terrace
a fish shop, paper shop,
pizza takeaway and hairdressers

And without fail
every Saturday night
we would meet there
at precisely 6:45

Me, and seven friends
that lived nearby
to stand at the steps of a shop
and kill time

We had no plans
but for reasons unknown
under no circumstances
was being late condoned

"The shop...6:45
...be on time"
and if anyone dared
to come at 6:49

It was SLAPS
with three free hits from everyone
that's a slap to your bare hands
times twenty one

In June it stung
but in January....well
you better hope to go numb
before your skin cracks and swells

And nobody spoke
of the pain it provoked
our suffering cloaked
under insults and jokes

Each of us broke
we chipped in for chips
the moonlight bounced
off our oil-glazed lips

We laughed into the night
like howling wolves
we feasted together
and went home full

Just young lads
with nowhere to be in life
but the steps
of the shop at 6:45

THIS TOWN

This is for anyone
in a small town
Always forgotten
and never called out

You probably know
how living in a bubble feels
Me too
but I'm just glad that bubble's Huddersfield

They say you become a
product of your environment
So then, are our ambitions
dictated by the size of it?

See, in my small town
we are guilty of small mindedness
We fall into a rut
and live and die in it

I try broaden horizons with
my words, I hope I help with this
'Cause I know there's a young kid
there who struggles to think big

But if I can open a door
I might show them there's more
So wherever I'm going
I go there as a spokesman for...

...THIS TOWN
where you can love it and hate it
You could destroy and rebuild it
but you couldn't replace it

It's not a place that you go
it's a place you end up
And I guarantee you fall for someone
that your friend does

It's all love
or at least it's trying to be
In the H - U - double D -
E- R - S - F - I - E- L - D

Our parents worked in the mills
we're cut from a different cloth
Putting my town on the map
for every time they missed us off

MAKING TEA IN HUDDERSFIELD

ME:	FRIEND:
Alright?	Alright?
Yupta?	Nowt
Brew?	Gonthen
Bag in?	Out

REASON 3

...BECAUSE YOU SEE THINGS DIFFERENTLY TO OTHER PEOPLE

GIRLS CRY ALL THE TIME

Have you ever noticed
How much girls cry?
It's not once or twice
It's all the time

But boys never cry
Well, in fact, maybe
We do when we're young
But I mean, like, babies

Or toddlers, perhaps,
But, of course, that's fine
And we've grown out of it
By let's say, age nine

Unless we get hurt bad
And it did us real harm
Like we cut a leg open
Or broke an arm

We might cry then
But that's normal right?
Or maybe if a friendship
Ended with a fight

Or if someone close had
Just passed away
Might cry then
And for the next few days

Or next few weeks
Or months or years
But that doesn't really count
That's a different kind of tears

Alright the only other time
We might cry, I'll admit
Is if we liked someone
Real hard, and it was legit

And we went out together
And had fallen in love
And then out of the blue
They said we should split up

Might cry then
In secret, alone
But does it really count
If nobody ever knows?

Or if we win
Something we really wanted to win
Or if we lose
Something we really wanted to win

Or if a piece of music
Was so moving
In our belly we felt
A volcano brewing

Causing a mountain of emotions
To suddenly erupt
So powerful, it pulled
Water through our tear ducts

But that's the power of music
We never **cry**-cry

Alright, wait, I might
Be telling a little white lie

'Cause when Mufasa died
Simba had to hide
And he returned to the pride
To learn Scar lied

You had to cry then
That was proper deep
So for that one
I give no apology

And we might cry when
We marry our life partner
Buy our first house
Or we become a father

And wave our child off
At the school gates
Or years later when they
Move out and graduate

Buy their first house
And marry their life partner
Have their first child
And make us a grandfather

There may be tears then
But that's justified
We NEVER shut ourselves away
Just to cry

Unless we feel sad
And can't explain why
But yeah, have you noticed
How much girls cry?

PLAYGROUND OBSERVATIONS

At school, I used to stand in the playground
And make observations as I looked around

I thought, people are quite like animals too
And the playground is sort of just one big zoo

For starters, there's fencing surrounding the grounds
Like cages to make sure that we can't get out

The overwhelming sound of everyone talking
Is as loud as a swarm of a thousand birds squawking

Kids mount the climbing frames gymnastically
And swing themselves bar to bar like chimpanzees

Some jump through hop-scotch squares like kangaroo
Some just sit and eat all day like pandas do

A group of girls dressed up in pretty pink coats
Just stand around on the field like flamingos

At the water fountain kids gargle and slurp
Like thirsty warthogs, only stopping to burp

A young kid trips over, all his friends laugh
As he struggles to stand like a baby giraffe

Some bigger kids, hide at the back of the grounds
Mischievous, like meerkats they keep a look out

The ones who play football run like they're cheetahs
With eager eyes open as wide as a lemur's

Playground supervisors are like zoo keepers
They round us up and send us back to our teachers

We roar, we growl, we screech, we howl
And I sit and watch like a wise old owl

SKIN

You don't really think
of skin as an organ
let alone your largest
and maybe most important
it covers each corner
and coats every curve
protecting your bones
blood vessels, and nerves
the pathway to both
pleasure and pain
from sweeping feather
to cold sharp rain
a patchwork quilt
of moles, marks
wrinkles, blisters
pimples and scars

fingerprints
make it your own
custom suit
that can't be cloned
it turns to dust
it peels, it flakes
and regenerates
in twenty-eight days
it heals itself
as if by magic
it bends and
stretches like elastic
how sad then when
we judge each other
by such a small thing
as its colour

THE STAGE

Remember the stage
is a mountain top
Not everyone
makes it up there

Some want the acclaim
the attention and fame
But when it's time to climb
they don't dare

Some sit at the bottom
and spend their life wondering
What the view's like
from the top

Some start on that journey
then turn back around
And learn
it's much safer to stop

But if you took the risk
accepted the challenge
And braved the onslaught
of the storm

Then the sound
of your worries and doubts
Weren't as loud
as the call from the stage to perform

BRAND NEW SECOND HAND

She opens the bag with excitement and wonder
A temporary distraction from tiredness and hunger
She reaches inside at the speed of a punch
Scrunches three shirts, and gathers a bunch

She whips them out from the bag to the ground
Separates, the blue, the striped, the brown
She's blind to the loose stitching, the frayed collars
The dog-eared cuffs, the sun-faded colours

Logos and name brands are of no importance
Her favourite is which one she'll feel most warm in
The clothes are my rejects. Worn. Used.
For her, second hand means brand new

REASON 4

...BECAUSE SOME THINGS PUT A SMILE ON YOUR FACE

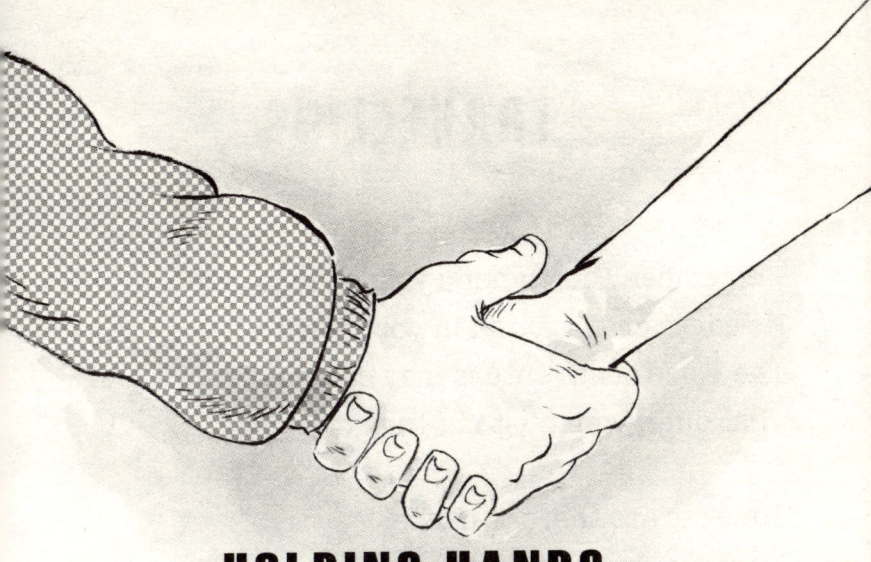

HOLDING HANDS

everyday our hands hold so many things
handles, keys, soap, sponges, drinks

buttons, food, phones, pens and pans
but none mean as much as other people's hands

we pick up, we switch on, we use, we play
we get bored, we put down, we throw away

but when two people's hands mould together
a memory is made that we might hold forever

TRAVELLING

Remember, the planet's your playground
Its edges aren't found in your town
The voice of adventure may call you
That offer, you must not turn down

Sun sets are there to chase
Keep moving and they never end
Follow the river's meander
Find stories at every bend

Wander where there are no footprints
Dance to the rhythm of the day
Squeeze all you can from your senses
Let them wash your worries away

Sail off toward the horizon
Don't make a plan to come home
Your curiosity's a compass
Your heart was intended to roam

BABIES ON BOARD

December 23rd, Kings Cross, London
Hundreds of travellers, bags in abundance

Bodies hastily cram onto carriages
Passengers fighting for seats become savages

Everyone's desperate, the atmosphere's tense
The heating is faulty, it's stuffy and dense

People have presents, boxes and cases
But they have no space, kindness or patience

And you, are carefree, beaming a smile
Peaceful, quiet and calm, meanwhile

An argument starts between two strangers
A woman barges through a group of teenagers

A desperate dad throws his coat to the floor
The instructor's tie gets caught in the door

A plodding pensioner clogs up the aisle
A stressed mum cries, her toddler runs wild

Sighing, tutting, crying, groaning
Shouting, whinging, whining, moaning

And you sit there, silent and still
Observing it all, contented and chilled

You're twelve months old, the youngest on board
Yet, somehow, you are the most mature

Really, you should be the most unhappy
You're missing your nap, you've filled up your nappy

But right now, you're the most civilised soul
And we're acting like a set of one-year-olds

To the baby on board, take my advice
Stay like you are for the rest of your life

RUNNING

Running is
freedom

Morning or
evening

Don't need a
reason

Sunny or
sleeting

In any
weather

Nothing is
better

Miles are
measured

In pain and
pleasure

Trainers on
concrete

Creating a
beat

Each rep-
itition

Natural
rhythm

STOP.
Wait to cross the road. There's an opening.
No, too close. This time, now, go again.

Running is
patience

Progressive
training

Heart beat is
racing

Deep medi-
tation

Incline
approaching

Slow down the
motion

Gravity
pushing

Pressure is
crushing

Pulling and
heaving

Suddenly
breathing

Isn't so
easy

Spluttering
wheezing

STOP!
Wait. Get my breath back. Chest opening.
Precious oxygen. Drink it in. Now. Go Again!

Running is
tiring

All engines
firing

Muscles
depleted

When the
fatigue hits

Pushing the
limits

Wanting to
quit it

Forty-three
minutes

Sprint to the
finish

and

STOP!

PRISM

The way that you
inspire me
Puts me in touch
with a higher me

Your words have always
been like a seed
The way that they
took root inside of me

You said the day I decide
to be who I'd like to be
Unimaginable change
will happen silently

I didn't quite believe
what you said but I tried to be
Open to it, you said "go and do it
give it a try and see"

There was too much
stubborn pride in me
But I think I get it

finally

Now on a night
when I try and sleep
Oh, the irony
I'm kept awake by a dream

And its only 'cause
I observed you for so many years
On my own
I'd have definitely swerved
Lost control
hit the central reserve
And exploded
but you keep me focused and set me to work

HEADPHONES

My headphones have always been a portal
To a world where I could feel immortal
The rhythm is hypnotic, I drift off
Gripped by the primitive drum pattern of hiphop

The boom-boom kaah, boom, buh-boom kaah
The music, the art, the truth in the bars
The beauty, the heart, the anger, the passion
The beats, the stories, the poetry of rapping

A shiver
Spirals up my spine
I was uninspired now my mind's
A kaleidoscopic eye

I hear colours
Neon frequencies
Piano chords and drum beats
Speak to me

Eyelids closed
Mind wide open
Time suspended
Attention unbroken

REASON 5

...BECAUSE YOU ARE GETTING OLDER

GETTING OLDER

Our lives become shaped
as silently
as clouds in the breeze

and time slips away
I guess them hours
were not ours to keep

And
oh
your
face
reminds
me...

At seven years old
he was king of the road
when he rode his BMX
bicycle on his own

And she

chased after him
proud and concerned
he pedalled with all he had
and remembered all that he'd learned

She shouted,
"Brake before you turn"
but he just wanted
to make the rubber burn

With no stabilisers
or hands on his shoulders
with pure joy, he yelled out
"Mum, I'm getting older!"

At fifteen
he was growing up fast
talking back, smelling of
smoke and growing a 'tache

And she

was working overtime
and had a short fuse
he wanted more freedom
she wanted more rules

he'd fallen for a girl
and had a chance to stay
alone at her place
while her mum and dad's away

she said, "No you'll come home
like you're supposed to"
he said, "I'm not a little kid,
mum, I'm getting older!"

At twenty-one
he was ready for the world
eager for success
independence and girls

And she

helped him pack his bags
when he moved out
and drive him 200 miles
down to his new house

Bubbling with anticipation
he unpacked
she said "If you ever need to,
you can come back"

He said "I appreciate that
but them days arc over
I need my own space now
mum, I'm getting older."

Then at thirty
he found himself stuck
single and broke
with his career in a rut

And she

listened while he told her
all his woes
with a patient ear for him
while they spoke on the phone

She said, "Well, we've finally
paid off our mortgage
so we can help with rent
if you have a money shortage"

He said, "No, I should
be a home owner
and I should get my own place
mum, I'm getting older"

By thirty-five
he had figured it out
found himself with a wife
a couple kids and a house

And she

babysat the children
every Sunday night
so he could have some
alone time with just his wife

He'd come back and tell her
all about raising kids
how he loved it but how
the pressure was changing him

How his hair's getting grey and thin
and when he showed her
they both laughed when he said
"Mum, I'm getting older!"

And at forty-six
he was always working
rarely with his family
so he saw it as a burden

And she

told him take
the pressure off yourself
he said "It's not as simple as that
see, I'm compelled

and the kids have gotten bigger
and I've paid for an extension
and I've booked a holiday
and there's the mortgage and the pension

and I'm not getting no younger
retirement's getting closer
and I can't afford to risk it, I mean
mum, I'm getting older!"

And she

just listened

She always did, but now
she's lost her vision

So listen
is all she can do these days

She smiles
and lines consume her face

And her body's
so frail, her hair is bright silver

And there's
ten conditions she takes pills for

And she
said, "we have come so far

And I know
you're getting older my dear...

We

all

are."

REASON 6

...BECAUSE THERE ARE THINGS YOU WISH YOU COULD CHANGE ABOUT YOURSELF

JEALOUSY

Jealousy's grip
is a hungry python
whose mind is on eating
it's squeezing the life from
my body, I'm weakened
consumed by the feeling
I'm trapped in its grasp
as I gasp, barely breathing

Jealousy's grip
is a persistent cold
an illness, I can't shake
or break from its hold
my temperature's high
my defences are low
it greedily feeds
off the strength that it stole

When I see somebody else
living my dream
a sinister side of my mind
starts to scheme
how can I take this
person down a notch?
how can I put myself
up in their spot?

But jealousy's grip
comes from my own palm
and in the end only
causes myself harm
held in the glare
of a green-eyed monster
but HE is not ME
just a selfish imposter

MY WORST HABIT

I would
Love to
Write a
Poem
That's a
Work of Art

But

My worst
Habit
Is I
Never
Finish
What I

HIBERNATE

I need to find a way
To hide away
For ninety days
Until the nights are light again
And the sun shines brighter rays

I need a private cave
An isolated
Silent space
Where I can stash supplies away
Stuff my face and pile on weight

I need a fire place
So I can bake
Beside the flames
And shelter from the icy rain
Why don't humans hibernate!?

EARLY RISER?

I wish
I could
Wake up
Early
But
I Never
Seem to

Even
When it's
Light
I am
Such a
Heavy
Sleeper

I hit
Snooze on
My
Alarm but
I just
Fall in
Deeper

I wish
I could
Change but
Maybe
I am
Just a
Dreamer

REASON 7

...BECAUSE THERE IS ALWAYS HOPE

FOR THE ARTISTS

I wrote this
For the artists, for the painters, for the poets
For the rappers, for the writers and composers
For the illustrators and vocalists
The world needs you more than you know it

And at your lowest
At your bleakest and darkest and brokest
At your weakest, when it's hardest to focus
And it all feels hopeless
The world needs you more than you know it

MISTAKES

I
Make
Mistakes

More than I make anything else
And I used to blame myself
Until my father told me he does the same

He still
Makes
Mistakes

He told me never undervalue
The lessons they amount to
And how they help your life take shape

HARD WORK

Remember that hard work pays off
And effort will bring a reward

You might find you need that reminder
Next time you're exhausted or bored

BLACKOUT

We were born
from the same dust
that the stars and the planets
happen to be made of
make of that
what you will
I'm just saying
our galaxy's built
with the same ingredients
we have in ourselves

humanity, animal, plant or mineral
down at the atomic level
everything begins to appear identical

I only say that to say this

on them days when your human condition
is just too much to live in

REMEMBER

your particular collection of atoms
could have scattered wherever
they could have turned into a badger
a tractor, a sweater
or a storm cloud on saturn
but they didn't they attracted together

and made YOU

what are the chances
that would happen again?
could you fathom the extent
of that miraculous event
to actually comprehend
everything that had to happen
you would have to track history
all the way back to Adam

or even further back
to the first atom
add 'em all up and your life
becomes the emerging pattern

but every day it's like
we lose perspective
we believe what we're told
and we chose to accept it

now we're thinking small
and we're falling in line
and we beg for crumbs
and we talk like it's fine
but it's far from fine
so as long as you have a heart and mind
see yourself in them
stars that shine

BECAUSE

we were born
from the same dust
that the stars and the planets
happen to be made of
make of that
what you will
I'm just saying
our galaxy's built
with the same ingredients
we have in ourselves

TOMORROW

Nobody knows
what tomorrow
will bring

It's a melody
waiting for words
to its song

I'm learning
the best thing to
do is to sing

Your heart out
and make it up
as you go along

REASONS TO
WRITE RHYMES

A COLLECTION OF RAPS AND RHYMING POETRY FROM
ROB BRADLEY

"Playful, poignant and powerful, Rob's natural craft and care of language comes through on the page, and makes you want to celebrate those poems out loud as well as hold them close to your heart. If you're looking for a reason to read rhymes, let alone write them, look no further than this book. What others spend a lifetime trying to get close to he makes seem effortless." - ***Harry Baker***

To arrange for **Rob Bradley** to visit your school, please email trevor@caboodlebooks.co.uk

ABOUT
ROB BRADLEY

Rob Bradley is a poetic rapper and storytelling songwriter. He has performed around the world, from basement clubs in New York to festivals throughout Europe, and collaborated with international artists along the way. He's built a solid fan-base and reputation as an astute lyricist, captivating storyteller and unrivalled improvisor, in fact he's a freestyle rap world champion. Rob visits schools in and out of the UK where he uses his rap writing skills and performance experience to help young people find and develop their voice and have fun exploring new creative ways to express themselves.